What's In Me

Hope you
Enjoy the
Adventure

Paul Guy Hurrell

First Published in 2022 by Blossom Spring Publishing
What's In My Fridge?
Copyright © 2022 Paul Guy Hurrell
ISBN 978-1-7396277-2-0
E: admin@blossomspringpublishing.com
W: www.blossomspringpublishing.com
Published in the United Kingdom. All rights reserved
under International Copyright Law.

CHAPTER 1

WAKEY, WAKEY!

"It's time to wake up Terry," said his mother as she popped her head around his bedroom door. Terry was already awake. He had been awake for the past thirty minutes just lying there in his bed, thinking of reasons not to get up and go to school.

Terry hated going to school. Not because he was bad at the work he was given by the teachers, in fact, Terry was very good at all his lessons except one, P.E. It wasn't that he didn't enjoy physical education, it was just because of his size. He went at a different speed to the rest of his class, much slower! He ran slower and he ran shorter distances than the rest of his classmates before he got out of breath. He found it difficult, if not impossible, to climb the gym apparatus, in particular the ropes and the climbing frames. Terry was so poor at them that his classmates would make fun of him regarding his lack of physical ability and so, Terry would try and shy away from participating in any of the lessons.

The only time Terry enjoyed P.E, if you can call it enjoy, was when it was football, and he would be in goal out of the way and there was very little running involved. While he was in goal, he was left alone for most of the game by everybody, there was no running for him, no climbing, although occasionally he would fall to the ground as if he were diving to save the ball. Then he would pick the ball out of the net and this would be him done until the next attack that resulted in a shot on target.

Today was Friday and that was the day he had P.E. This was also the day that Terry didn't want to get out of bed, Friday was his hardest day at school. Not just because of the P.E lesson, his hatred of this day was added to by all the name calling before school. At playtime, at lunch time and at afternoon playtime, Terry would be chased all the way home. This was the day that his sister Tracey finished reception early, at noon, so his mother wasn't there to walk home with him, and this was his protection, hence why Fridays were always the worst day of the week for Terry.

The name calling didn't just come from one person or from one group of kids, it just seemed to be from the nearest kids that could be bothered to poke fun at him. Terry was feeling alone, even when he was at school surrounded by all the other 530 pupils, and when he was at home, he was still feeling alone even though he was next to the three people in all the world that unconditionally loved him. His mum and dad, plus Tracey his little six-year-old sister.

Due to the sadness that Terry was feeling all the time, he rarely went out of the house to play. He would stay up in his bedroom and entertain himself, watching the television, playing on his PlayStation or completing his homework.

When he did venture outside of the house, he would take Tracey into the garden with him, but even with his younger sister with him, Terry always felt lonely and sad.

Terry would always feel on edge in the garden just in case someone from school would walk past and spot him and start to shout insults at him. When this happened it hurt Terry even more, because his little sister Tracey was with him and in his eyes, it was his job to look after and protect her, but when this happened, the only way he could protect her was to usher her quickly into the house, or into the back garden out of the way, while trying not to listen to the name calling. It was like being on a picnic and a thunderstorm comes and you have to pack up and run for cover before you get soggy sandwiches and runny cupcakes.

Tracey didn't really understand what was occurring, or what the words meant, or why she had to stop playing with her big brother and go inside. The only good thing for Tracey was once they were both inside away from the strange boys' heads that appeared above the wooden paling fence, was that Terry carried on playing with her and didn't run up to his bedroom away from everyone.

Terry just stayed where he was, lying in bed staring around his room, looking at the shadows that were bouncing off his toys from the beams of light coming in from around the sides and top of the curtains, from the sun shining in his room.

The bedroom door opened again and Terry's mum stepped inside the room this time. "It's time to get up sleepyhead," she said in a caring, quiet voice.

Terry rolled his head sideways to look at his mum and gave a halfhearted smile, more like a smirk while replying that he would get up. With this response she left the room, but left the door wide open as a reminder for Terry to get up.

As his mum disappeared through the open-door, Terry threw the quilt off the top half of his body and took a deep breath before sitting up. He swung his legs over the side of the bed and after a few seconds he lowered himself 20 cm to the carpeted floor before standing up and leaving his safe haven.

He went into the bathroom then went back into his bedroom and got dressed into his school uniform. After combing his hair looking in the small bedroom mirror, he headed downstairs into the kitchen, where Tracey was already sitting at the table dressed, and eating her breakfast of jam on toast. As Terry sat down at the table, his mum placed a plate with two pieces of toast smothered with strawberry jam in front of him.

While Terry was eating his breakfast, he forgot about going to school, he forgot about the name calling, he forgot about being chased and pushed to the ground, and he forgot about how sad and unhappy this made him feel.

It wasn't long before Terry had cleared his plate of toast, and all that was left on the plate were some crumbs and a small blob of jam that had fallen from the toast. All he could think about now was the day he was going to have at school and all the problems he was going to encounter, unless he could dodge everyone at school, this was now where his thoughts were.

Could he stay in at playtime, could he tell the teachers he wasn't feeling well at lunch time? Maybe he could hide during the afternoon playtime. All he had to do now was carry his plan out and the only time left to cover was on his way home from school to his sanctuary of his front garden gate, this was safe land for Terry. It was like witches that couldn't stand on church land.

CHAPTER 2

FATSUMA

Terry's mum took away his used plate and put it on the kitchen worktop, next to the sink for her to wash later. She left the kitchen and re-entered it carrying Terry's orange rain Mac.

Unknown to Mrs Birdsall this coat was the main reason behind one of the nicknames Terry had. The nickname that he hated, Terry's nickname started as orange, then they added fatty orange which later became Fatsuma. This nickname stuck and was still with him today. No matter where he was, he would hear "FATSUMA", even when he wasn't wearing the orange Mac.

One of the other names he was called was Birdpoo, or a variation of this, but this was only said or shouted when there were no teachers or adults about. There were other names they called him: fat boy, fatso, chunky, beach ball, greedy, balloon, plump, chubby, flabby, porky, pudding, bulky, tubby, dumpy, huge, porky, pudding, stout, roly poly, wobble and lard arse.

In the beginning Terry was able to ignore the name calling, but the longer and the more the name calling went on, the harder it was for him to turn a blind eye. All the name calling would make him sad and depressed. It got to the point where Terry was so upset by the name calling, that he wouldn't go out to play and he hated going to school.

CHAPTER 3

PACK UP

Mrs Birdsall was standing next to Terry with his orange Mac in her hand. Terry could see the coat through the corner of his eye, but he sat there staring at the table, at where his plate had been moments earlier.

Terry was trying to ignore his mum, but he knew that he had to go to school, so he took hold of the coat without moving his head to look at her. His mother left the kitchen.

The three of them walked in a line towards the front door with the smallest first, as they walked Terry zipped his coat up. When they got to the door Terry stopped and turned around and pushed past his mum and before his mother could ask what he was doing, Terry shouted out that he had forgotten his packed lunch, "it's in the fridge," his mum shouted after him.

This was a tactic he was using to slow down his journey to school. As he took hold of the fridge door handle and pulled it open, he heard his mum's voice shouting that they would wait outside for him.

He put his left hand inside the cold fridge, but instead of him taking hold of his plastic lunch box, it felt like something grabbed his hand tightly instead and started to pull on him. The more Terry pulled against the force, the stronger the pulling got and the tighter it gripped on his hand. The next thing Terry knew he was being lifted off the kitchen floor, his body was being pulled up, his whole body was leaving the floor and he was heading into the fridge.

The whole of the inside of the fridge seemed to dissolve and was replaced by a cold white light, which looked like fog, which he couldn't see through. The force was pulling him in faster now. Before he knew it, his whole body was inside the fridge and the door closed behind him. Once the door slammed closed, Terry seemed to start following the light. Faster and faster, he was falling, and Terry was screaming in fear as he plummeted.

His body was tumbling over and over, faster and faster, until there was a sudden pop sound and a jerk, and the falling slowed down to a gentle floating. Still going down, the speed and tumbling had stopped, his orange mac had filled up with air and acted like a parachute and was slowing his descent down.

He was now floating and all the panic in his body had fallen away, he was now enjoying himself just floating. He was looking around himself trying to find somewhere he knew, but all that was around him was whiteness.

Then suddenly, the white started to give way to a pinkish light, it was like threads of a spider's web hitting his face. Terry was wiping his face trying to pull the sticky threads off, but each time he cleared his face, more threads replaced them. As the threads stuck to his head and with the action of him falling, the threads were blowing above his head which looked like his hair was sticking on end, making him look like a mad professor.

Once again, the pinkness went just like the white light went and Terry could see white ground below him. As he floated lower, he could see bits of brown sticking up out of the white and he was feeling cold now and the lower he got the colder he became.

Then there was a jerk and a slush, Terry wasn't moving any more he was now standing on solid ground even though it was a bit mushy and cold under his feet.

Luckily for Terry he had put his boots on that morning, so there was no leakage over the tops of his footwear or through the lace holes.

Slowly, Terry took a few spongy steps, it was like walking in mud, but Terry carried on walking towards one of the brown posts that he had noticed, whist he was floating downward.

As he reached the post Terry stopped and put his hand on it to balance himself and to catch his breath because the walking was hard. He looked around, then suddenly a piece of the post he was holding onto broke off in his hand. He rebalanced himself and examined the lump in his hand, turning it one way then the other and it was at this point that he realised that the lump was made of chocolate or he thought it was, but he didn't try it. Terry just dropped it on the ground and with a plop it sunk under the surface.

Terry carried on walking, but he found the trudging hard and had to keep having to stop to get his breath back. As he stood leaning against one of the chocolate posts, he could hear a strange noise, a clunk, a whirring and chattering with a loud pulping, along with hissing and a pisst.

As he looked around, he could see in the distance a small grey dome shape heading towards him. As it got close the noises from it got louder, until in front of Terry there was a large grey dome, with a smaller glass dome on top.

Around the bottom of the grey dome there was a small furry trimming, which were multi coloured balls. There were red, yellow, green, blue, orange and white, no two colours the same were next to each other.

Just above the coloured fur balls there were small silver pipes, each furry creature had its own pipe and just above two of the single pipes merged into one pipe, this pipe was thicker than the last one. All the way up the pipes merged into thicker ones until they all ran into one large pipe. This large pipe ran just below the glass dome and went around the back like an exhaust pipe.

As Terry looked up at the glass dome, a pair of large eyes appeared, but they seemed to be floating. Then there was a loud noise and a stern voice coming from the machine. "Who are you and how did you get here?!"

Terry just stared at the floating eyes, and didn't reply. Then the voice came again asking the same two questions. Again, Terry didn't answer, not because he didn't want to, it was the fear of who or what he was going to speak to that worried him. Then the eyes sunk out of sight into the glass dome.

There was a large hissing, which made Terry take a step backwards, then the hissing was followed by a clanking noise and then a rumbling, then a section of the dome moved outwards to reveal a strange looking creature sitting on a purple chair which was on the end of a metal arm.

The creature had a yellow furry body, two brown legs and matching arms, and was wearing gloves and boots which looked too big for where they were being worn. It had a lighter brown head and two stalks sticking approximately 15 centimeters above its head. Each stalk had a blue eye at the tip which seemed to be the set of eyes that were just floating in the dome. The creature had a large red beak, which looked too big for its face.

The creature kicked his heel against the metal brass plate under the cushioned seat he was sitting on, the brass plate fell open and out dropped a step ladder, dropping to the ground in front of Terrys feet.

"I am called Polly and I am lord of all the land you see and stand on. I am the first lord of Tendale, the ruler of Weedorn and Keeper of all that has gone before," he said, as he walked down the steps, trying to look regal, but he slipped down the last three rungs of the ladder and landed flat on the ground. He stood up as quickly as he could hoping that the fall hadn't distracted from his cool entrance in front of Terry. He dusted himself down and carried on as if nothing had happened. "The keeper of all you can see," he repeated.

Terry was now feeling nervous and scared, but was thinking *keeper of what I can see*, which was nothing at all. As he was looking over Polly he managed to mumble "I am Terry." The next question was how did you get onto my land? Terry tried to explain to Polly, but he didn't really know or understand how he got there himself.

After a short discussion, Polly told his frightened friend that he needed to go to see the Blue Queen in the city of hope and she would be able to help him get back home. Then he climbed back up the steps to his chair, the ladder retracted behind him and the metal arm and chair with Polly sitting on it went back into the Gobulator. There was clunking, whirring and a large hissing along with a chattering.

Then it moved off to the left, so Terry thought he better follow, and he set off walking behind.

CHAPTER 4

THE SMELLY JOURNEY

Terry found that as the Gobulator moved forward, it left a clear space behind, making a solid pathway for him to walk on, rather than the gluey, mushy, stuff he had been walking on since he had landed in this strange land. The furry multi coloured skirt around the bottom of the dome were Gobies and all they did was eat, trump and poo, which made them great at making pathways around the land.

As the dome moved on a small section at the rear would push out two solid brick like objects which were placed down on the ground like kerb stones, these would hold the white creamy stuff back, until Terry had walked past. The pipe end was just above and in front of Terry's head and now and then there was a loud trumping noise and a terrific arduous smell came out of it, which he kept walking into.

The smell was so bad that on the first couple of occasions this happened, Terry was nearly sick at the side of the pathway. The longer the journey went on, the more he seemed to get used to the smell. He would move out of the direct firing line of the pipe and move to the left or right, just to get a break from the smell.

He had moved his walking line to the right of the end of the pipe. So, it was only when the Gobulator veered to the left or right, that Terry got caught out and got a blast in the face of the smell, which would make him then move to the other side of the pathway to try and escape the stench.

Then all of a sudden, the Gobulator stopped, and a loud and large plume came out of the end of the pipe, which seemed to stick around Terry's head, making him dance about and wave his hands frantically trying to waft the smell away from his nose.

The metal arm came out of the side of the dome and Polly walked down the dropped step ladder. Terry walked from the back of the vehicle to find himself standing next to Polly, who was standing in front of a pair of large blue wooden gates. There was nothing other than the gates and the gate posts, there wasn't a wall or a fence, just the gates.

Polly volunteered to be the guide for Terry, announcing that he was the best guide in all of the land and that he would lead him to the city of hope. Then he explained that they needed to go through the gates and this would lead to the city of Hope.

Terry looked and felt confused not understanding the reason why they had to go through the gate when they could just step around them.

He moved slowly to his left so that he could see around the tall gates, he couldn't see anything on the other side of the gates, just white ground with brown stakes, the same landscape as to what was behind them. He was confused because there was no boundary wall and nothing beyond the gates.

He couldn't understand why they had to go through the gates when there was no wall blocking their way. Polly looked back staring into his eyes and said, "in this land not everything is what it seems."

Polly then stepped forward and knocked on the wooden gate with a hardy knock, three times on each gate. After a lot of creaking a voice asked, "what do you want?"

Polly replied, "we would like to enter the city of Hope"

"What is the reason why?" came the gates response.

"To get my friend home."

Terry became sad and happy at the same time, sad because he was missing home and happy because for the first in a very long time, someone had called him their friend.

The gates went on asking questions and

Polly replied to them all and then with a loud crack the gates opened wider and wider, until Terry could see a great city through the open gateway. Terry again went to the side of the gates and just as before there was nothing to see only wilderness, but looking back through the gates the city was there.

Polly started to walk towards the opening and shouted for Terry to follow him, which he did. When they reached the other side of the gates they started to close, until there was a bang and the gates were shut.

To the left of the gates there was a huge wall standing over five metres high and was coloured yellow, it seemed to carry on forever. Terry couldn't see the end of it, it just carried on out of sight and when he turned to look at the right of the gate, it was just the same in that direction. Then he noticed in the distance a lot of different coloured lights.

The lights were bouncing up and down and coming towards them. As they got closer, Terry could just about make out that the object's coming closer were round in shape, they were like balls only with two arms and two eyes. Each time they bounced and hit the ground, they changed colour.

Polly shouted over to Terry to stand still while they got past, which they did quickly off into the distance. There were about thirty of them, some brushed against Terry and one or two of them bounced over his head.

Polly explained that they were called Boingers and that's what they did all the time, but they are harmless as long as you stand still and don't get in their way. Terry watched as the coloured balls disappeared in the distance.

When he turned back around, he found Polly was walking down the road towards the city, so he quickly caught up with his friend.

As they walked along side by side, they chatted and Polly explained about the magic city and the journey to it and Terry asked as many questions as he could think of, all of them relating to the land that he now found himself in and ways for him to get back home to his family. Then it was Terry's turn to fill in Polly with his background, the only question Polly asked was why. Why was he bullied, why was he called nasty names?

As they walked side by side Terry started to fall behind. His new companion was leaving him behind, so he started to walk faster, but he wasn't closing the gap, so he got faster and faster, until he was trotting, but still Polly was further away in front.

Then Terry looked down at the ground and he realised that the path under his feet was moving just like a treadmill in a gym, so no matter how much faster he ran the faster the ground under his feet moved with him, there was no catching up with Polly. At this point, Terry did the worst thing he could do and he stopped running, but as we all know when you stop on a treadmill, the treadmill will carry on moving. At this point the treadmill threw Terry off backwards landing him flat on his front.

Polly looked behind him and saw what had happened and started to laugh. He was still laughing when Terry picked himself off the floor and caught back up with him. Polly tried to say, "I told you nothing seems to be what it is in this magical world," but it was hard for him to get the words out because he was laughing so hard. But eventually he got them out and they carried on walking zig zagging around the moving ground as they walked forward, Polly guided them.

It wasn't long before they came to a halt at the foot of a wooden sign post, which had four direction pointers on it and written on them were the words Forward, Backward, and the other two had Sideways written on.

Terry asked, "which way to go?"

"Forward," was the reply, "it's always forwards if you are unsure which way to go."

So, they marched on past the useless signpost.

The next sign post they came across was identical to the first one, only this time the four direction pointers read Creepy Wood, Evil Trees, Mean Wood, Scary Forest. They stepped forward only by one step, and the wood just appeared in front of them.

All Terry could see were trees and the grass on the ground. There was no other vegetation, but as they walked past the first line of trees into the woods it got darker. Terry looked back from where he had walked, he was looking towards the shrinking light, in his head, he was saying goodbye. At the same time telling himself that he wasn't afraid, but he was.

As Polly and Terry walked deeper into the wood the less light was coming through the wood's canapé, but there was enough light to walk by. Then Terry noticed there were little lights in the trees, little glimmers and the more he looked at them the more he realised they were slowly moving or was it his mind playing tricks thinking there was movement in the shadows? Terry was more frightened now, but Polly just carried on walking deeper into the darkness of the wood.

Then something touched Terry on the head, which made him jump throwing his hand up in the air, trying to move or squat whatever it was that was touching him. He started to run and soon caught up with his guide and walked so close behind him that it was as if they were marching in close formation like soldiers.

Then suddenly Polly stopped, Terry bumped into the back of him nearly knocking him over. As Polly went forward to steady himself, he bent over and touched the ground with his hands. Terry saw the reason why Polly had stopped so quickly, in front of them there was a sheet of twinkling lights which were blocking their way. Polly moved to the left and Terry shuffled behind him peering over his shoulder.

The blanket of twinkles moved with them blocking them, so Polly moved to the right and the curtain moved back, each way they moved the twinkles moved with them, it was like each move was a mirrored image. Then Polly shouted "run" and he set off running straight at the blanket. Terry thought they would run in the opposite direction of the twinkles, but no, Polly was running towards them. Terry stood there watching as Polly disappeared, it was now that he thought he better follow Polly running into the twinkling blockage.

The blanket of twinkles seemed to be all around him now. The more he pushed them aside, the more there seemed to be. Terry's hands were frantically pulling and shoving at anything that came into contact with any part of his body. Then he tripped and fell onto his hands and knees, but he didn't try to get up, he just crawled along the floor on his knees at speed, moving away or just crawling over what was in his way.

As Terry's head emerged into the sunlight, he could just make out Polly's figure standing in front of him. It was hard for him to focus due to his eyes not yet adjusted after coming out of the darkness of the wood. The sunlight was bright and directly behind Polly.

Then Terry tried to stand but he could not, his legs seemed to have something rapped around then. He tried again to stand, but fell over again, his legs were now out of the wood. And as Terry looked at his lower body, he could see two long black twinkle strands wrapped around his ankles.

Terry started to panic and started shouting "get them off me!" While wriggling his legs, trying to break free from their hold. Polly stepped back towards Terry, laying on the ground and took hold of both the twinkles with his hands and unwrapped them from his legs, and then placed them on the ground, letting them go. On their release they quickly slithered away from Terry and back into the dark wood.

"They are just twinklers, they can't harm you," Polly informed Terry as he held out his hand to help him get up off the floor and back onto his feet

"So why is it called the Mean Wood," asked Terry

"It's all in your head, it's just shadows, wind and twinklers, your own imagination does the rest."

When Terry got to his feet, just in front of him was a new wooden signpost with three direction pointers that read "This Way, That Way and Other Way."

"Which way should we go now?" asked Terry, still looking up at the signpost.

"Well, there's no point going that way is there and the other way is out, so I think it is this way," came the reply as Polly started to walk away.

"That way?" asked Terry.

"No not that way, this way," came the reply.

"Which way is this way?" enquired Terry.

"It's this way we need to go," Polly pointed out.

"Why is it that way?"

"It's not that way, it's this way," replied Polly.

At this point Terry was totally confused and decided it was best just to follow Polly and ask no more questions.

They walked off in the direction of the pointer that was stating *This Way*, both in silence. After a while Terry started to sink, he looked over at Polly for help but he was already down to his waist. They both looked at each other and started shouting for help, but the more they shouted the more they sank.

They had sunk up to their waistline. They tried to crawl out of the ground that was trying to swallow them, but they couldn't stop the sinking. It got so bad that their hands were under the ground, and they couldn't get them out to help themselves escape the trap. They looked like they were on their knees as they struggled trying to get back on top of the soft ground.

Again, the more they moved the lower they went, they were now up to their chests, one of Terry's hands broke free so he brought it down on top of the ground and grabbed hold of a handful, but he couldn't lift his hand up, it was stuck again now the ground was under his chin. Terry looked over to find that Polly had disappeared, and it wasn't long before he was surrounded by darkness as he went under.

Then there was a rumbling and a pressure under Terry and then he felt himself moving upwards, then the darkness gave way to sunlight. And there in front of him was Polly, who was riding a green, ground worm and a similar creature was under Terry.

The worms were about six metres long with two eyes, one month and there were six different coloured tails. The worms would go in the air then dive down going underground, but they made sure that their passengers didn't get fully submerged.

The worm's movement was like a rodeo horse and Polly and Terry were the cowboys. Up and down, they went holding on for their lives not wanting to fall off and end up back in the ground and sinking again.

The worms carried on along the path making sure their passengers didn't fall off and sinking back under the ground. The further along they went on the backs of the worms the more fun the rides became, until it got to the point where they were both shouting out in enjoyment, both of them laughing from the ride of fun.

Then the worms started to slow down and eventually came to a stop. They had come to rest at the foot of a wooden signpost. The worms laid flat on the ground and both Polly and Terry stepped off their rides. Polly walked along his worm to the head and bent down and while stroking it he smiled and said, "thank you." Both worms turned and dived underground, out of sight.

The signpost read *My Way*, *Your Way*, *Their Way*, and *Our Way*. "Which way shall we go now?" asked an inquisitive and slightly weary Terry.

"It's my way of course," came the response and after the last conversation regarding which way to go, Terry thought it best not to question his judgment this time. Off they went again with Polly taking the lead as usual. As they walked along, they discussed the events of their journey, the fun, and the fear and all their different emotions.

Then they suddenly stopped walking and talking, because in front of them there were a number of twisters, cones of wind, which seemed to be dancing about in front of them, blocking their way. At this point one of the twisters moved forward heading towards them both.

This was when Polly shouted run. Terry turned and started to run away from the twister that was heading towards them, but Polly grabbed his arm and told him to turn around and run towards the twisters.

Not believing what he was hearing, he stopped and turned to see Polly running in the other direction. Polly running towards the twisters, he was weaving in and out and ducking under any of the twisters that came near him. On seeing this Terry set off running, following Polly dodging the ones coming near him.

Then Terry stopped dead and just glared in front of himself as he saw Polly rise into the air inside one of the funnels of wind. Terry at this moment felt lost, let down, afraid and alone as his leader, companion, and most of all his friend, was five metres in the air going around and around inside the funnel of wind, as the twister revolved.

Terry was so angry that he ran at full speed

towards the twister that had imprisoned his friend. Terry ducked the first twister, ran to the left then to the right dodging more of the oncoming cones. Then directly in front of Terry was the twister that encased Polly. As he got to the foot of the twister, he took a deep breath and leapt into the air, straight into the twister next to his friend.

They grabbed each other tightly and pulled themselves close so they were hugging as they were spinning around. Then suddenly, the turning slowed down and then stopped, both Polly and Terry started to release their grip.

Then they looked up to find that the top of the wind cone was starting to fold downward, lower and lower it went, until the folds were at head height. Then what was left of the cone started to change shape and elongated itself, then two small lumps rose in the middle.

There was a wobble and shaking, making the two occupants fall backward leaving them sitting on the raised lumps, like two chairs.

The wind cone started to move off gently taking Polly and Terry on a smooth ride, as it moved forward the other twister cones moved out of its way and let it pass through them, without any buffeting or bumping.

The wind transporter came to a halt in front of a pair of blue wooden gates. Then the cone started to change shape again, making the seats they were sitting on change to the shape of a slide. Suddenly, Polly and Terry started to slip down the slide through the floor of the funnel. As the pair reached the bottom of the slide, they were lifted into a standing position just in front of the gate. The wind then morphed back into the cone shape and blew off the way it had come from.

CHAPTER 5

START OF THE END JOURNEY

Terry stood looking up at the large gates and then he realised he was alone. He looked around and then he noticed the Gobulator parked at the side of the gates, just where it was left. Polly was walking towards it with his head down.

Terry shouted over to Polly and asked, "where are you going?" On hearing Terry's voice, Polly stopped and turned around and looked straight at him and said in a sullen voice, "I have to leave you here."

"But why?" asked Terry solemnly

"I just have to it's the rules, I am only your guide and I have brought you to your destination. I am not allowed to take you into the city of hope, you need to head to the palace and ask the Blue Queen for help."

"Aren't we back at the same gates we started

at?" asked Terry.

"Yes, like I said, this place is magical and strange, but you need to go forward to find your way home, I can't help anymore." And without another word he turned around, walked over to the Gobulator, climbed the steps and sat back into his chair on the end of the metal arm.

Terry watched and waited thinking and hoping that he would stop, turn around and say something else, but he didn't. The metal arm retracted back into the dome and with a lot of noise, the Gobulator moved off slowly, leaving a track behind it as it ate everything in its way.

He watched until he couldn't hear the noise and then he couldn't see it in the distance. Terry stood there feeling lonely and afraid, and not sure what to do now. Then there was a deep-toned voice asking, "what do you want?" On hearing this Terry turned himself around, only to find there was no one there.

Terry than realised he had heard the voice before. The voice came again asking the same question in the same tone and manner. Terry took a deep breath and replied. "I want to go home."

There was a clicking, clanking and a rumbling, then the gates started to swing open. The wider they opened; the more Terry could see beyond them. He could see a picture full of buildings and a road in front of himself, framed by the gate posts.

There were small buildings, large buildings, tall buildings and wide buildings. In the distance there was a large golden building that had a blue dome on top of it and on top of the dome there was a tall spire, with a flag fluttering in the breeze.

This wasn't like the last time the gates opened, when there was nothing behind them, just emptiness. Terry stepped forward and walked through the gateway. Once inside, he stopped and turned his head to watch as the gates closed behind him, locking him in. At each side of the gates ran walls, which went out of sight in the distance.

There was only one way to go now and that was forward. As soon as Terry took his first step, a car pulled up at the side of him, frightening Terry a little due to its sudden appearance. The car was bright orange, there were no doors on the car and on the roof, there was a blue box with a flashing word that read "Taxi."

"Can I take you anywhere, Sir?" came a voice from within the taxi. Terry bent down and looked inside, but there was no one driving the car. There was a small screen at the front with a smiling face displayed on it. Again, the voice asked Terry the same question. Terry noted that the movement of the mouth onscreen didn't match the spoken words.

Terry stepped inside the taxi and sat down, the next words instructed Terry to fasten his safety strap, but it came out elongated "pleeeease fassssten yoooour saffffety strrrrrrrap."

Terry found both ends of the strap on the bench seat he was sitting on and pushed them together, and as soon as they clicked, the taxi moved off at speed, throwing Terry backwards against the backrest. The taxi lurched forward then downward picking up speed.

Due to the steep downward movement, Terry was thrown forward. The safety strap held him and stopped him from tumbling into the front of the taxi. Then the taxi jerked to the right, then the left throwing him both ways, it went upwards and then Terry found himself upside down as the vehicle did a loop de loop. Terry thought to himself how different the world looks from this position.

Sitting there he realised that all the movements the cab had done, the road and the buildings around him all moved with the taxi. Then the taxi headed at speed towards a house, aiming straight at an upstairs window. Just as Terry covered his eyes in fright at the immediate impact, at the last second the window opened and the taxi went through it, going through somebody's bedroom then out of the other side through an opposite window.

Then again, a sudden drop. The cab was now running at speed along the side of a white paling fence, towards a street lamppost. Unlike the window, the taxi veered off to the left at the last moment, missing the lamppost, now heading towards a lamppost on the other side of the street, only this time the taxi went up steeply over the top of the lamppost and dropping down sharply on the other side of it.

The taxi was picking up speed as it headed towards the pavement. Closer and closer the pavement came. As it came up, Terry saw that in the middle of the pavement there was a manhole cover and the taxi was hurtling directly to it, and just before the taxi hit it, the manhole cover opened up dropping downwards and the taxi shot through the opening.

The taxi leveled out once it was underground. All that Terry could see were small lights at each side of his head flashing past him, the wind from the speed was blowing in his face. Then suddenly, the taxi started to climb upward. The speed started to decrease and then there was a blast of light in front of him as the taxi emerged back in the street, Terry's eyes adjusted themselves now he was back in the street.

This was just like being on a roll-a-coaster ride, only instead of being at the seaside it was in the street. Terry was buffered left, right, up and down, going through houses, over lampposts and trees, around bushes and underground.

Then all of a sudden, the ride came to a halt with the voice saying, "yooooou arrre herrrre siiiiiir, Iiiiii hooooope yoooooou enjooooooooyed yoooooooour riiiiiide." Terry was shaken, but he did enjoy the ride.

Terry unfastened the strap across his waist and stepped out of the taxi. He stood there for a moment making sure he was ok and to gather his thoughts. While he was standing there, the taxi moved off slowly. Terry was thinking why it didn't go at that speed when I was in it. He watched as the orange taxi turned right and was out of sight.

CHAPTER 6

THE QUEEN

Terry turned right and found that he was standing at the foot of a wide expanse of steps. The steps climbed up in front of him, they were so high that Terry couldn't see what was above them or where they led to. At this point he took a deep breath and placed his right foot down on the first step, but as he did his foot sank a little into the step, but not too far down.

He lifted his left foot and because of the sinking of his right foot, he placed it next to it making sure he had his balance. Then he carried on walking up the steps, making sure that each step he took he stood with both feet on them for safety and balance.

Terry didn't realise he had got to the top because he had been concentrating so much on making sure he hadn't lost his balance and fallen all the way back down.

Standing at the top of the steps he looked out in front of himself. Across a short golden precinct there was a pair of golden doors, these doors were as big as the blue wooden gates he had walked through some time ago at the boundary, where he left his friend Polly. He found that the surface of the precinct was just as spongy as the steps and he kept wobbling and falling to his knees, but he soon got the hang of lifting his feet higher than normal and plunging them down, it was like walking in mud or deep snow.

It didn't take long before he was stood at the base of the golden doors, so he knocked with his right hand and to his surprise, the doors swung open, so he stepped inside.

The large room was empty except for a large chair at the far end of the hall. Terry slowly stepped forward and he looked around the large room, taking in how grand the hall was and then something made him look down. There in front of him was a white line painted on the tiled floor which reached from wall to wall. On the far side of the line were the words "do not cross," and on the nearest side of the line were the words, "wait here."

As he waited, there was a noise from either side of him and at each end of the white line, there were doors in the walls, which opened wide and soldiers started to march out of them. The soldiers marched towards Terry and just as he thought they were going to walk in to him and knock him over and he would get trampled, the two lines of soldiers turned sharply and headed towards the chair at the far end of the hall that Terry had noted already. After a noisy couple of minutes, the soldiers stopped and were stood to attention, facing each other across the divide.

The two long lines of soldiers were holding spears in their right hands and in their left hands they were holding a shield. Each soldier was dressed the same in shining armour and had a long red cloak that hung over their left shoulder and down their backs, just stopping before they touched the shiny floor. Each soldier was wearing a silver helmet with blue ribbons hanging down to their shoulders.

There must have been one hundred soldiers in each line. Terry looked down the lines and at the end he realised what he thought was a chair, was in fact a throne and there was now someone sitting on it. The queen was sitting on it, she was dressed all in blue.

She had blue shoes and wore a blue dress, which matched her blue face and blue hair. Terry waited there not knowing what to do or say, the only thing he knew was that the longer the silence went on, the more nervous he became and the more nervous he got, the longer the silence seemed to go on.

Terry stood on his side of the line where it read "wait here". Nervously shuffling his balance from one foot to the other, then he turned to the nearest soldier on his left and quietly said "hello." On this the soldier turned to his left and loudly and sternly repeated the sole word of *hello*, which was then passed along the line of all the soldiers on the left until it got to the queen at the end.

Then there was a clicking sound coming from near the throne. Terry could see things moving in the distance near the queen, then two small creatures known as Tippytappies, came from behind the throne. Albert and Herbert walked up the void between the two rows of soldiers towards him. As they got closer Terry could see they were carrying something between them, plus there was a tapping noise which was getting louder, the closer they got.

The two Tippytappies were pulling what looked like a trumpet on one wheel, which was making a squeaking noise as well. As they became closer, Terry noted that sticking out from the bottom of their trousers was a cluster of what looked like twigs from a tree and each twig had a boot on it, and this was what was making the tapping noise on the tiled floor. There were approximately fifteen boots on each foot sticking out from the base of their trouser legs, this made them appear to be floating over the floor and not walking on it, their hands were the same, just twigs.

They both stopped just short of the white line on the floor, with the words "do not cross." They both bent down and pulled out two stabilizing legs from the wheel, then they walked away back towards the throne and the queen.

Then the voice of the queen came out of the cone, "why are you here" the voice asked, Terry looked around then replied out loud, "I want to go home." Again, the soldiers passed this information down the line as before, but this time it was the right side of the line of soldiers that past the message along.

The queen's voice came again from the cone, asking Terry to speak into the cone. Terry took a step closer to the cone and as he did, the two end soldiers on each line stamped their feet on the floor and presented their spears as a warning not to move any further forward.

Terry leant forward making sure that his feet didn't cross the white line, but his head did. This seemed to be ok for the soldiers, who withdrew their spears and returned to standing to attention.

An instruction from the queen was to speak into the cone, this was followed by the same question, "Why are you here?"

"I want to go home," came the same reply, only this time Terry spoke into the cone.

Then she asked how he got there, so Terry explained about the fridge and him meeting Polly and him bringing him to the gates. The queen responded by saying that Polly was probably the best, honest and fun guide there was.

The conversation carried on for a short while longer between the both of them. With the queen stating that she could help Terry return home, but he had to do something for her first, and that was to go to the Dragons Lake and bring some dragon juice. Terry didn't know anything about dragons or dragon juice, but he wanted to go home, so he agreed to do it.

As Terry left the palace and wobbled down the steps, a taxi as before pulled up appearing from nowhere, so he stepped inside. Climbing in the rear again and getting the same greeting as before and also the same instruction to fasten the safety strap, which he did, the taxi moved off at speed.

The journey wasn't any different than his last ride in a taxi, up, down, left, right and loop de loop, underground. Terry enjoyed this ride from the off and was a little bit sad when it came to a halt five minutes after it had started.

There in front of him was a sign sticking out of the ground in front of a privet hedge, with an arrow pointing to the left and two words. "Dragons Lake," under the black arrow.

Terry set off walking and after a short distance the privet hedge stopped and he was stood at the banks of an orange lake and in the middle, there was a large brown mound. There were two signs, one read "Do Not Feed the Dragons" and the other sign had only one change of wording and that was Become, so this sign read "Do Not Become the Dragons Feed."

He unclipped the bottle from his belt that had been given to him when he was leaving the palace. He bent down and reached into the orange lake, dipping the bottle into the thick liquid and letting it flow into the open neck, until the bottle was full. Before taking it out and fastening the lid back on the bottle and clipping it back onto his belt.

Then he noticed that the brown mound in the middle of the lake seemed to be moving. Terry stood there not able to take in what was happening, but the mound was starting to unfold and expand. Then after a couple of moments Terry realised that it wasn't a brown mound, but it was two dragons intertwined and this was where and how the dragons slept.

As they untwined the two dragons stood up on their hind legs and outstretched their wings, which cast a shadow over Terry as he looked up at the magnificent but frighting site of these two beasts. Terry couldn't decide whether he was frightened by the dragons or excited by them, because he had never seen dragons in real life before, they were only mentioned in fairy tales and books.

Then there was a loud roar from both dragons. Terry knew now how he was feeling and that was frightened.

The dragons settled down to a standing position, both were staring at Terry, who was now crouching and looking at the ground in fear, he was hoping that if he couldn't see them by not looking at them, they couldn't see him? He then felt a wind hitting the top of his head, only this wind smelt bad, then there was a pause, then a hard voice.

The voice was asking who he was and what he wanted. Terry slowly lifted his head up to find himself eye to teeth with one of the dragons, who had lowered and stretched his head over to were Terry was standing. The teeth of the dragon were nearly half the size of Terry's head.

Terry was trying to turn his head away from the beast because the smell of its breath was putrid. The smell was that bad it was making him wretch; Terry was doing all he could to stop himself from being sick. It was the worst smell he had ever smelt, it was even worse than the smell of his little sister Tracey's dirty nappy, when she was a baby.

CHAPTER 7

DRAGONS

Both the dragons were standing tall, one of them was leaning towards the now nervous and frightened little boy standing on the bank. It asked again the same question, only this time a little more sternly. Terry dropped his gaze again so that he was facing the ground, not because he was frightened, which of course he was, it was due to the smell from the dragon's mouth.

"I want to go home," he replied, quietly and nervously. The dragon moved forward a little, which Terry didn't want.

The dragon enquired, "you want to go home?"

"Yes."

"Where is home?"

"27 Farm Hill."

"I think I would rather eat you little boy, than to let you go home"

Now worried, Terry raised his head and stared into the left eye of the large dragon. "I want to go home to my mum and little sister Tracey,"

"But your unhappy at home, aren't you?"

Terry was surprised by this statement; he had no idea how the creature knew this. Terry kept silent and the dragon squinted his eye and tightened his lips and moved that little bit closer, that was when the dragon inhaled. Terry felt that he was being dragged forward, and when it exhaled, he felt he was being pushed back.

The other dragon leant forward and whispered in the dragon's ear, "remember when we couldn't find Scorch the panic it caused, the upset and the sadness, luckily for us we found him."

"What are you saying, Matilda?"

"We have to help this little person get back home, to his family," she continued.

"Ok, if you say so."

As he spoke, four baby dragons' faces appeared from behind the second dragons head where they had been hiding "Let me introduce you to my family," this came in a softer gentler voice than before, but it still stank.

"This is my wife Matilda, I am Theodore and these are our babies, Fire, Burnt, Scorch and Ember."

Terry could see the eight eyes staring at him, then they all climbed over their dad's forehead and down his long nose and one by one they jumped off their dad's nostrils and flurried downwards. Their dad introduced them. "Fire, Burnt, Scorch and Ember." One of them landed on Terry's head.

"That's Fire, he hasn't yet totally grasped the art of flying," informed Theodore.

Over the next twenty minutes Terry and the four baby dragons played in the grass and sometimes in the orange lake, with the dragons flying up in the air and then plunging into the lake before flying out again - even Fire was doing this after a while.

After a while of Terry getting splashed and dripped on, he decided to get into the fun more and stepped into the lake himself, leaving his boots and coat on the grass bank. It wasn't long before he had lost his balance and ended up sitting down and been surrounded by the orange liquid, but it didn't matter that he was soaking wet, he was having fun and forgot about going home and how unhappy he was.

The two parent dragons were so pleased that their four babies were having fun and looked so happy. Even Fire was having fun and her flying was getting better and better, the more they played. After they had called an end to the fun and games, they both told Terry that they would help him get home, but first they had to dry him.

The four baby dragons all flew into the air and hovered in a virtual line at the side of Terry and started to blow little flames out of their mouths. They were placed at the right distance from Terry so that the flames didn't touch him and burn him, the heat from their breath was drying him out just like a set of hair dryers.

The dragons started to move slowly around their target, making sure that every part of him was dry.

After he was dry, Terry put his coat and boots back on, but all the time he couldn't think of any way that they could help him get back home. Terry had already got the liquid from the lake that the queen had asked for, so Terry explained why he was there and all that was left was for him to go back to the queen, to hand it over.

The two adult dragons spoke to each other and then they insisted that they take him back to the palace. After Terry had said goodbye to Burnt, Scorch, Fire and Ember, he climbed onto the neck of Theodore and from a running bumpy start they sawed up into the sky. Once in the air, the ride became smoother. This journey back to the palace was a lot better and easier than taking a taxi.

The dragon circled the palace twice then landed on the forecourt. Terry climbed down off his ride and went and stood in front of Theodore and thanked him for his help. Theodore thanked Terry for his help and fun he provided for his kids, then he started running and flapping his wings again, he took off into the air and as he circled the palace, he gave a roar and a jet of flames shot out of his mouth in front of him for approximately twenty meters.

Terry watched and waited until Theodore was out of sight, then he turned and went through the palace doors for the second time that day.

It was just the same as the last time Terry entered the large hall. The two doors opened one on each side of him and the same soldiers came marching out and lined up in rows of two, standing to attention just as they did before.

Terry stood there watching, taking the spectacle in. The marching, the ridged formation and the standing to attention. The noise that was all around his ears quickly died, giving way to the silence as the soldiers stopped moving. After the noise had ended, the two small men came out from behind the queen's throne again, and while they were getting the hearing cone ready, the Blue Queen came out of a side door just across from the throne. She walked across the throne room; her footsteps made no sound on the hard tiled floor.

By the time she had reached her throne, the two aids were dragging the cone towards Terry. Just as before the aids pulled the stabilizing legs out of the wheel, once the cone was fixed in position, they then returned to the throne without saying a word, standing at each side of their queen.

"Have you got what I asked you to get for me?" enquired the queen.

"Yes, I have it here," he said, unclipping the bottle from his belt and holding it out in front of himself as an offering.

The nearest soldier on his left stepped forward and took the offering out of Terry's hand and returned to attention in his line and then passed it onto the next soldier with a swing of his right arm. The bottle was passed down the line of soldiers towards the queen, just like the first time Terry had spoken to her on his earlier visit, one soldier at a time.

The aid on the queen's right took the bottle from the last soldier's hand and went around the rear of the throne, only to emerge seconds later carrying a silver tray with a glass resting in the middle of it. Terry could see that the glass contained the orange liquid that he had brought from the dragon lake.

The queen reached out and took hold of the glass and held it up to the light, then slowly turned it several times while she examined it. After doing this the queen brought it down to her lips and took a little sip of the liquid. Then she looked at it again in the sunlight that was beaming through the palace windows, the queen repeated this three times more.

On the last occasion the queen drank the glass dry. After drinking the liquid, the queen returned the glass back to the tray, placing it upside down to show that it was empty.

The aid went back around the back of the throne and returned empty handed. At this point the queen sneezed and her hair turned orange, then she sneezed again, and her face turned orange. There were further sneezes and each time the colour of orange fell down her body replacing her blueness, until she was orange from head to toe.

He stood on the spot mesmerised, he watched the queen change colour from blue to orange. He had never seen anything like this before. The only time he had seen anything that came close, was when his little sister Tracey had painted her face in different coloured stripes, and because it wasn't water-based paint, it took over two weeks for her mother to wash it off. Tracey had to go to nursery looking like this, much to the amusement of the rest of the other children in her day nursery. This was how she got the nickname of Bow which was shortened from Rainbow.

Terry's attention was brought back into the palace when he heard the queen's voice coming out of the cone. "Can you come here young man?" Terry looked behind, thinking that someone else had entered the hall behind him, but then he realised that the queen was asking him to walk forward.

He slowly, but tentatively moved forward and came to a standstill just in front of the white line on the floor. Terry lifted his foot up extra high to step over the white line, it was as if the line was a high obstacle in the air, not flat on the floor.

Once over the line, Terry looked at the two rows of soldiers and this time they didn't move, so he walked on slowly between the rows of guards. He could see their eyes moving as he walked past them, but nothing else moved, their heads were motionless, Terry now found himself standing within three feet of the queen and her two aids.

He didn't know if the queen herself was different or had she just changed colour, because he never saw her close up before. The only thing he knew was that her hair, face, and dress had changed from blue to orange. Again, Terry's mind was brought back into the here and now, by the voice of the queen.

"Now young man, you have done what I asked of you, so it is only right that I the queen do what I said I would. Can you remind me what it was that you asked of me?"

"To go home back to my family." Terry was thinking about his mother, father and his little sister Tracey. His chin rested on his chest, his shoulders dropped and hunched forward, with sadness. He spotted the tip of the queen's right shoe wasn't the same colour as the rest of her. The queen stopped talking realising that Terry needed a few moments with his thoughts, he wasn't listening anyway.

Terry lifted his head up and looked the queen straight in her eyes and informed her about the blue tip on her shoe. To which the queen lifted her right foot a little off the floor and pulled her dress up slightly, so that she could see for herself the shoe tip and with a little shake of her foot from left to right, the tip turned orange. Without a word, just a smile on her face, she placed her foot back down onto the floor next to her left foot, bringing both shoe tips parallel to each other making sure there wasn't one in front of the other.

"Young man, now that I am properly dressed, you want to go home to your mother and little sister, this is right is it not?" the queen asked.

"Yes."

"Even when you aren't happy there," enquired the queen.

Terry was shocked by this statement and wondered how the queen knew about his life back home. This wasn't the first time it had been mentioned in this land and for a brief moment the memories of being bullied came flooding back, and not realising, Terry's face looked sad.

The queen quickly realised this and said, "I didn't mean to upset you and I am sorry. Now young man, let me help you get back home."

On hearing this Terry forgot about the bullying and a smile returned to his face as he understood that the queen was really going to help him, and with excitement in his voice he said, "yes please."

"Before you return home, I want to remind you of some things. Number one, things are not always what they seem. Number two, keep going forward. Number three, all journeys have a start and an end, the bit in the middle is down to you. Number four, take a deep breath first. Number five, this is a magical place. I must thank you for getting my liquid and helping me change. I have been blue for so long, I can't remember what it is like to have more than one colour in my life, but I will make up for it now thanks to you Terry. Now if you go through that door to my right, it will take you home."

The queen pointed over to her right and Terry looked along at her outstretched arm to where it was pointing, he could see a wooden door to his left. Terry thanked the queen and walked off towards the door, on reaching the door Terry noticed that there was no handle or knob, so he couldn't open it.

Terry turned around to ask the queen for help, but there was no one there. The queen, her two aids and the two rows of soldiers had all disappeared. The strange thing about the empty room was there was no sound made as they left, which Terry couldn't understand.

He turned back to face the door and that had now disappeared. There was just the palace room wall panelling, which started at the floor and went up to the plastered ceiling. Terry stood there just staring at the wall where the door was a few moments ago, then Terry heard the voice of the queen in his head saying, "this is a magical place and things are not always what they seem."

Terry then heard Polly's voice saying, "keep going forward," then "take a deep breath." He took a deep breath and stepped forward towards the wall. As he walked forward, he put his hands out in front of himself and instead of the resistance of the hard panelled wall, there was nothing, his hands just sank into the wall.

Terry kept walking forward and when he looked down, his feet had disappeared into the wall and his hands were suddenly cold, very cold. Then his face was in the wall followed by the rest of his torso. Then there was a falling feeling. Terry was going down faster and faster and all around him there was a whiteness, as he fell Terry was getting colder and colder, then the falling stopped gently, and Terry was back home in the kitchen holding the handle to the fridge door.

He didn't have a clue how he got home and how he was holding the fridge handle; all he knew was this was the last thing he remembered before his crazy journey started.

Then he heard a familiar voice, so he turned his head while still holding the fridge door handle. It was his mother asking, "how long are you going to be? You will be late for school if you don't get a move on."

Terry thought that he must have been dreaming or something, but he did open the fridge door slowly with anticipation, and while the door was a jar, he slowly moved his head around it so that only his left eye could see inside.

The inside of the fridge just looked like it always had; salad on the bottom shelf, meats, both fresh and processed in packets on the middle shelf, and on the top shelf there were dairy products, including cheeses and butter and there in between was a plastic see-through lunchbox. In the box Terry could see that there was a sandwich wrapped in tin foil, a cartoon of juice and an apple, this was Terry's packed lunch.

This time Terry reached into the fridge with his left hand while still holding tightly onto the handle with his right hand. He quickly grabbed his lunch, pulling back his hand as quickly as he could, and then slammed the door shut. He left the kitchen and the house as quickly as he could.

All the way to school, Terry held his little sister's hand tightly.

CHAPTER 8

NEW BEGINNINGS

Terry said goodbye to his mother and Tracey as he left them at the gates to the lower building, where the infants and primary classes were located, which is where Tracey went Monday to Friday.

Terry tapped Tracey on the top of her head. He said goodbye to his mother walking away quickly before she could kiss him farewell. Normally, he would give a mumbled 'goodbye' before walking off.

Terry walked up the path to the blue gates of the senior school. Just before he entered the gate, he took a deep breath and then made his way into the playground. For some reason today felt different than every other day at school, he felt happy about going in.

He walked past the first group of children and not one of them called him names. He walked past the next group, again not a word. The next big test was waiting just in front of him. It was Max the school year bully. Just as Terry got level with him, Max stepped into Terry's path blocking him off and said, "where are you going, Fatsuma?" Terry looked him in the face and took a deep breath and replied, "into school, so please let me pass."

"The fat boy wants to get past, does he?" was his response.

"Yes, I would." Again, after taking a deep breath this time Terry took a step forward, moving closer to the bully.

Max was surprised by the boldness and response of his victim. In fact, this might have been the only time Terry had spoken back to Max in all the years that he had tormented and bullied him.

Max took one step closer, trying to further intimidate Terry. Today Terry didn't move, he just steadied himself and stared Max in the eyes. This for some reason made Max more unsure and as usual in the only way Max knew, he lashed out by pushing Terry hard on the shoulders with both hands. Terry took one step backward to steady himself and to stop him from falling over backwards onto the ground.

By this time Terry found himself opposite the bully and surrounded by some of the other pupils from the playground, who had gathered around after realising what was happening. Terry wasn't feeling frightened, he was still feeling happy, so he stepped forward again and said, "Maxwell, why don't you just pack it in acting like this all the time?"

Before Terry had finished speaking, he could hear some of the other children around laughing and repeating Maxwell's name. The other kids only ever knew him as Max and now found it funny to find out that his full name was Maxwell.

This enraged Max, who lunged at Terry who was pushed backwards again due to the force, but Terry soon regained his composure and stopped himself from going any further back. At the same time that Max was pushing Terry, he was calling Terry *fat boy, piggy face and fatsuma*. Terry just kept smiling then he said, "why don't you just grow up."

Max carried on calling names, but no matter what he called Terry, he kept smiling, which made Max more and more angry. Then Terry broke his smile. "You know Maxwell I can lose weight, but you will always be a bully."

This was the point that there was more laughter from around the circle of on-lookers and this made Max even more aggressive. He was just about to punch Terry in the face, as this is what bullies do, when they have lost any arguments, they resort to violence. Only on this occasion the circle started to part and emerging through it was Mr Knight the English teacher, who was on playground duty and had spotted the gathering and gone over to investigate what was causing it.

Mr Knight stood behind Terry and put his hand on his right shoulder tightly and asked, "what is going on here then?" Terry didn't speak, he just lifted his head to his right to see who was behind him.

Max responded to the teacher. "Nothing Sir" he said. At the same time as unclenching his fist.

"So then let's break up this little meeting, shall we?"

The circle quickly broke up and the children walked away. The teacher kept his hand on Terry's shoulder, gently holding him where he was. Max turned away, still angry, but he did walk away reluctantly, thinking to himself, *I will get you later.*

Mr Knight turned Terry around to face him. Then he asked if he was alright, to which Terry responded "yes, Sir." He was then asked if he needed to report anything, but this was rejected by Terry, so he was released from the teacher's grip to go into school for the morning registration.

The first lesson of the day was English literature with Mr Knight. Today he wanted the class to relay a story about themselves, each pupil had no more than ten minutes to recite their stories.

There were five classmates picked before it was Terry's turn. Terry marched to the front of the class, which was something he wouldn't have done before. He would have been reluctant to speak, always sitting at his desk, never mind at the front of the class, but today he was different.

Terry started to speak, loud and clear his voice wasn't shaking like it normally did and he relayed his recent adventure in the fridge, from start to finish. Because the story was so good and presented so well, Mr Knight let him carry on beyond his allotted ten minutes. Terry finished telling his story after twenty-three minutes.

As Terry finished, the rest of the class and

Mr Knight erupted in a spontaneous applause. The only person who didn't clap was Maxwell the bully, who was still thinking about getting even with Terry.

Terry returned to his desk and sat down with the clapping still ringing in his ears. He felt so good within himself, he had never felt like this before, he didn't want this to ever end. Mr Knight stood up and made a speech stating how good the story was and how well it was presented. He praised it so highly that he rated it the best story he has had the privilege to hear in all his days of teaching from any of his pupils. He then made the class stand up and applause again, and he even made Maxwell stand up and clap. Begrudgingly, Maxwell did as the teacher ordered.

When Terry was walking out of school at the end of the day, a lot of the other children were complimenting him, not just on his storytelling but also about him standing up to Max in the playground. Terry didn't want this feeling to stop, he wanted the day never to end.

He left the school grounds and walked home, taking his usual route home, still smiling and happy. And as he was walking across the wooden bridge over the stream, he noticed a figure at the start of the ginnel to Farm Hill Crescent. Terry could make out it was Max waiting, but he didn't care. He didn't stop walking and he didn't turn around to find an alternative route home, he just carried on walking towards the bully.

Max was leaning on the chestnut fence that ran up both sides of the ginnel, in front of the hawthorn hedges between the two gardens which formed the ginnel boundaries. He pushed himself off the fence and stepped into the middle of the ginnel blocking it off.

When Terry got within three metres of Max, he stepped to his left, but Max moved across to block him, so Terry went to his right, again Max moved across to block him again. Then the abuse and threatening started. "Right then, fat boy, thought you were being smart earlier with all your mates around you and the teacher there to save you. Let's see what happens to you now, when you are by yourself." All that Terry was thinking at this point was that they were not his friends, they were just other children from school.

Max lunged himself at Terry, pushing him to the ground. As Terry laid flat out on the ground, Max got on top of the outstretched body of his victim, kneeling over him. But just before he could punch Terry, there was a loud roar and a whoosh sound from behind the fence. Max turned his head to look behind himself and saw the fence and hedge behind started to move and shake, then there was an explosion of fire.

While the smoke was settling down, Theodore the father dragon stepped through the swirls of smoke and over to the feet of his friend Terry. Theodore looked down at Max who couldn't believe what he was seeing. Then the four baby dragons flew out from behind their dad, Fire, Burnt, Scorch and Ember.

Max rolled off Terry onto his back and then scrambled to his feet, at the same time Fire sent out a small jet of fire from his mouth, which hit Max on the bum, making him jump in the air with pain, then Burnt did the same. Max ran away shouting and screaming as the four baby dragons fired their flames like darts at him as they flew behind.

After a short while Theodore called his children back. They all turned around and formed a line in the sky, then returned to their father, who was talking to Terry.

Terry thanked them all for their help and within minutes they had gone. Walking back through the smoke, Terry walked home still smiling and happy. He walked through the ginnel, along Farm Hill Crescent onto Farm Hill Square, then up the second ginnel onto Farm Hill and into his house at number twenty-seven.

Terry never again had any trouble from Max. In fact, Max kept away from Terry for the rest of their school days. Terry over the next year lost weight and became a lot more mobile and enjoyed all kinds of sport. He was very good at football and enjoyed his life. He also made a lot of friends!

The End

Dedication

This is my first book and the only person I can
dedicate it to is my wife Beverley,
who has always been at my side.

About The Author

I was born in Leeds, Yorkshire, in 1960 to a single parent family. I am the youngest of five siblings. I was brought up on a council estate and my family had very little, just like many other families on the estate at the time.

I attended two schools as I grew up – Bentley Lane infants/junior School and then Stainbeck High School. School was always hard for me, mainly because of my absenteeism. I wasn't ill, it was just my mum didn't send me (empty nest syndrome). Looking back at my school years, I think I probably spent more time at home than I did at school!

I officially left school in 1976 and my first full time job was making special mirrors, the ones you see in pubs. I didn't last long there before I got bored. I was forced to take a job back at Stainbeck High School repairing desks. While there I met my wife, Beverley. We have two wonderful grown-up children and three grandchildren.

I worked for Leeds City Council, in the Housing section for 22 years, before retiring. Since retiring I have the time to carry out one of my first loves, writing. My first children's books is called What's In My Fridge, published by Blossom Spring Publishing.

www.blossomspringpublishing.com

Printed in Great Britain
by Amazon

84724147R00058